BLISS EXPERIENCED NOW

Bliss Experienced Now

Susan Fratis Penny

Copyright 2018 by Susan Fratis Penny. All rights reserved.

Cover Art: "Wheel of Life" by Mary Angela Penny

"Amir" by Marjorie Knettle, who contributed the concept of Amir's vest and pocket.

"Mayan Woman" by Avelina Leanos, drawn from her knowledge of Latin Culture.

Published October 25, 2018

ISBN: 9781729071403

Dedication

Liz Irwin published her first book, a Memoir of her childhood, at age 86. Upon learning that I was inspired to begin publishing my books when I was 67 and have continued to do so until the present at almost 80 years. She truly transformed my life by her example.

Toby Johnson has been my friend, teacher and editor for 40 years and we have communicated by daily long distance phone calls for 30 years. His close personal relationship with Joseph Campbell has enriched the quality of this project.

Matthew James Penny is my eldest grandson. At age 20 he has developed his interest in Greek Myth to include the study of myth in general. His knowledge and ideas have contributed greatly to the development of my personal myth. It goes without saying, sharing our passion and interest in myth has created a bond for which I am most grateful.

Susan Fratis Penny

Introduction

This book began as a series of journal entries kept as part of an eight week series of Jungian sand tray therapy sessions with Chris Tsuboukura, originally a colleague in the Department of Psychiatry at California Pacific Medical Center, Pacific Campus.

Sand Tray is often referred to as a process of "waking dream." The client choses objects from shelves of miniature figures to place in a "sand tray," a box of sand similar to a kitty litter box in size and configuration, thus creating a scene of images from the imagination of the client and then analyzed or interpreted by the client and therapist. The natural elements of earth, fire, water and air are represented and reflect the world in which we exist in the creative representation. Often, as in my experience, the client keeps a journal recording the process of the progression of the unfolding story or "waking dream."

The therapy and journal happened in the summer of 1975. I recently found the journal, having forgotten about it. To my surprise I realized the discovery of creating a peaceful refuge from a then difficult and painful time had actually taken place in my life in the years following the my sand tray process. I decided to write the narrative as a personal myth, as influenced by watching Joseph Campbell's interviews with Bill Moyers on Netflix in the summer of 2018, my 80th year.

I decided to make the myth into a chapbook to be shared with companions of my journey in those 80 years and to integrate experiences of the years 1975 until 2018 with the memories of years preceding the therapy. I had the help and inspiration from many I knew during my life experience but I especially want to acknowledge the help, input and inspiration of two people.

The first is Toby Johnson, my friend, colleague and teacher for 40 years, with whom I have shared daily long distance phone calls for more than 30 years. He has been an able and patient editor for all my books and has provided extensive, if not magical, assistance in those projects. He was a friend and mentored by Joseph Campbell and as such has been a valuable resource in the inception and execution of the idea of fulfilling the creation of my own personal myth.

The second person is Matthew James Penny, my eldest grandson, whose interest and research into Greek Mythology has given him an educated appreciation of the discipline of understanding and interpretation of mythology. Sharing our interest and affection for myth has brought special joy and satisfaction to this project. Sharing this collaboration at the end of my life, with him at the beginning of his, is something I appreciate enormously.

So I give you this piece of my history and acknowledge that all of you have had some part in the development of my life story told symbolically but based on real experiences. Thank you.

Agape,
Susan Clare Fratis Penny

Inspiration for the focus of the book

Mary Varney Rorty, PhD, a friend from Barnard College, and now an eminent Philosopher and Bioethicist, supplied the word synthesizing the focus of this book:

SOTERIC

Coincidentally, as I was researching myth for *Bliss Experienced Now*, my friend and editor, Toby Johnson, PhD, brought to my attention a version of *soteric* he had used in his book *Finding Your Own True Myth*.

Here is the quotation from Toby's book:

> …the verification principle for religious doctrines is not whether they are true, but whether believing them results in… *soteriological experience*, i.e., the sense of being saved from whatever the religion says you need to be saved from or for—nirvana, heaven, Abraham's bosom, Jannah, Paradise (p. 115)

—Bliss

1. City of Origin

Alice was walking down a steep hill with tall buildings and cement sidewalks. All along the way, Alice knew something was not right.

At a glance, the city looked calm and inviting. All appeared to be as if it were a nurturing community. But the streets of the city were lined with armed men assigned to keep conformity by authoritarian control. The citizens were told the soldiers were there to keep peace, but the reality was that they were forcing compliance and punishing diversity. Among those citizens were children wounded by cruelty and abuse.

Alice felt out of place, like she was living in a city filled with strange and unpredictable realities. She had been told about a girl named Alice who had experiences in a place called "Wonderland" and also had experiences as if living through a looking glass. Alice understood that point of view and from her earliest memory called herself "Alice." She no longer remembered her given name.

The only comfort for the inhabitants was in brief relief from sporadic kindness from members of the community. Otherwise they existed in a hostile world. Those moments of kindness rarely lingered and were too often interrupted by change of heart or abandonment. Endless failed trust could be expected and the most familiar response was to retaliate against aggressors.

Alice was part of that community since early in her life. Her attempts to cry out against what was perceived as unfair was heard as angry disruption. There was no place for childhood mistakes and false starts. There was shame in considering the status quo as not quite right.

Alice and her companions were considered ungrateful and disobedient if they tried to rebel. Since they were guilty they had to be punished and made to realize the error of their ways in questioning the situation they were experiencing. The concept of mercy seemed to elude the sensitivity of the elders. Forgiveness for challenging the situations experienced was not ever considered an acceptable as a response.

Alice always felt out of place and tried to hide—to withdraw from the bullying she experienced. Alice dreamed there existed something else and spent hours imagining herself in another world. When she grew older and had children of her own, she could not imagine conforming to the norms of child rearing that she had experienced. She determined to leave that city and set sail to a land she had observed in the distance and dreamt about visiting from her earliest years.

One foggy and especially oppressive day Alice determined to embark on her journey to the distant land and began walking toward the pier where the ship to the distant island cast off and she would begin her journey, hoping to find a way to have a better life.

2. Boarding the Boat

Alice increased her speed as she got closer to the beach at the bottom of the hill. At middle age, she was pale from lack of sunlight in the city. Following her were Jaime, a son about nine years old, and Angela, a daughter, about eleven. They were both dressed in play clothes. With them was a Golden Retriever. Sadie. They dawdled behind their mother so the distance between them and her grew.

Alice could see a ship sailing toward the shore that was her destination. Looking around her she observed the people on the deck of the ship. For years she had watched the ship sail from an island perceived miles away. Alice had dreamed of leaving the barren land.

As she came toward the bottom of the hill Alice saw a soldier standing with his gun by his side. He was far from Alice but she was afraid he would stop her from boarding the ship to continue her voyage—that he would make her interrupt her determination to leave the city.

Behind the soldier was a blue dinosaur a little larger than Alice. The animal had his hand raised as if to hold back the soldier if he came into her territory or to deter her from boarding the ship. When Alice came to the gangplank, the dinosaur came close and spoke to her, "I am called Amir and I have come as a guide in your journey to the new land. I have lived through many incarnations and bore witness to many individuals' evolutions."

Alice noticed he was wearing a vest, which made her curious.

She asked him. "I have never seen a dinosaur wearing a vest. Is that usual for you?"

Amir smiled and answered, "I am not an ordinary dinosaur. I told you I have been a guide for many with a calling to discover new horizons. That is for each on a journey for various purposes and destinations. I have a vest to carry supplies that might be needed along that journey for those I guide. Along with practical objects there are magician potions ready for any unexpected situations for which they might be needed." Alice felt reassured by his answer— acknowledging that he was prepared for any contingency along the journey.

As her first impression, Alice liked Amir. She felt secure and intuitively accepted his company. He was calm and reassuring. Then he pointed out a snail sitting on a piece of driftwood on the beach. It was not struggling, not climbing, just sitting near the sandy shore taking time to rest. Amir pointed the snail out to Alice, indicating to her that this was one of the lessons she would encounter along her journey. Amir said, "You need to slow down to incorporate some information from where you are."

Alice replied, "It is as though I have run a race and am still geared for it. But the race is ended. I am programed for the struggle and I have trouble adjusting the fine tuning, the slower momentum different from running the race."

Alice wondered where the man was she had seen earlier along the street where she gad been walking. She saw he was standing and observing her. Then she noticed there were people on the ridge of the hill watching their friends arrive on the boat nearing the shore. She thought it will take awhile for the passengers to get used to the more crowded environment of the city.

Alice stood at the seashore waiting for the boat to come into the harbor. She had a nagging feeling pulling her back. What about her children? She thought to herself, "If I go back to get them there is the chance the boat will leave without me. I can't go back now."

She had never left then before and the idea of leaving them behind made her a little anxious.

Along with the lingering pullback was also the anticipation of going to the island; Alice became perplexed. Alice waited with Amir as the passengers coming from the island disembarked and progressed into the city.

The weather was warm. A breeze was blowing, pushing the boat into the shore, its sails flapping in the wind. Alice realized the time had come for her to embark. She glanced back at her children and the landscape she was leaving. The presence of Amir gave her courage to move forward to the deck of the boat and she was grateful for his presence.

Alice was no longer sad at leaving the children but had a feeling of adventure to find what she would discover. As the boat pulled out the sails were swelling. She saw the figures in the city grow smaller—particularly her children by the shore. Sadness lessened in knowing somehow they would be together again. The sea was calm but the wind blew gently and the ship moved swiftly to the other shore.

Alice and Amir saw a man on the shore. In the distance they could see a tall figure. Alice had seen no one except Amir on the ship and was glad to see someone else waiting, especially since it appeared to be the man Alice had seen before leaving the city. Alice was filled with questions about what would transpire having finally arrived, but felt reassured having the company of Amir.

3. Arriving on the Island

When Alice and Amir walked down the gangplank to the shore of the island, trees and foliage surrounded them. They were struck by the lush foliage as contrast to the bleak surroundings of the city.

Amir asked Alice "Now that we have arrived, what are your observations of the voyage her?"

Alice thought a moment and then said, "Somewhere on the boat I knew someone was steering but I did not see anyone. It was like with an airplane pilot. I watched the dolphin in the pond filled with seashells and he was smiling at me as if to welcome my passage on the ship to the island. I saw a walrus on a large rock and a seal clapping his fins, there were alligators in the water, but I knew they would not hurt me while I was on the boat and protected by you. There was so much sea life—a real contrast to what I had observed in the city."

Then Amir asked, "Now that you have arrived on the new land, what are your first impressions?"

"There is so much natural beauty here—it is very different from what I was used to in the city. Are there other people here? I saw a young man by the shore from the boat. I thought I recognized him from watching me walk down the hill to the boat before leaving the city.

"In the distance, while we were landing, I saw the tall figure of a shadowy woman dressed in clothes from antiquity."

Just then a man of about thirty years, of medium height and build with brown hair and a spare beard walked out of the nearby trees and approached Alice and Amir.

Alice asked, "Aren't you someone I saw in the old land?"

"Yes, I came here not long before you. I watched you walking toward the boat and wondered if we had the same destination in mind. How was your trip?"

Alice began to understand somehow and was glad to find someone traveling a route similar to hers and to share the journey. She replied, "It was all very smooth. There were dolphins and seals and I was not afraid. How did you get here?"

"I can't remember. I was walking along the shore and realized I was lost in the woods and could not find my way back. I followed many paths which grew narrower and narrower—paths that were overgrown with plants. Then it was becoming dark and cold. I found a cabin with an open door. There were chairs, a bed and food. I drank some strangely flavored drink which made me very sleepy and I slept until dawn." Then he continued, "In the morning I walked outside and discovered a church on a hill." He pointed to the church, and behind the spire of the church Alice saw the figure on the hill. Alice began wondering what she would discover and learn on the island she had waited so long to approach.

Alice learned the young man was named John and she thought he might have some of the answers to the questions she had about the new place where she had arrived. She decided to query him.

"Did you see a tall old woman dressed in clothes from ages past? I saw a shadowy figure like that from the boat. I think I see her on the hill in front of us. I would like to find her to learn more about her but I am not sure I am safe from the Indians I heard live on the island. Are they dangerous?"

Amir suddenly replied, "Yes, there are Indians but they will protect you, not harm you."

The man added. "I was protected from the Indians in a sacred space by the church. I heard an angel talk to me and say the Indians would not harm me. Because those who come top the island on a quest of discovery are not touched. You too are safe if you remain focused on discovering lessons to be learned here to lead you to self truths."

Alice had more questions about what John had learned from the angel he discovered near the church on the hill.

Alice asked again, "Did she tell you how you got here?"

"She wouldn't tell me, only that I had arrived on the island and that I would discover many lessons I would learn traveling inland from the shore. She told me you would be coming for example. How did you know to take the ship?'

"For a long time I thought about it. But one day I saw it coming to the shore of the city in which I lived. I walked to the pier and just felt drawn to it as though that was what I should do. I thought of each person I was leaving before I left. My lifetime went by in thinking and remembering. When the time came that I left, I did not say good-bye. When I saw the boat coming I just went down to meet it. Then I met Amir and I had the courage to get on the ship with him. I am happy you are here to meet me."

Then there was a lull in the conversation and Alice asked, "What am I supposed to do now?"

Amir spoke up, "There is no 'supposed to'; it's up to you to do what you think your journey leads you next."

Alice turned to the man, "Will you come with me?"

"No, I am going back to the cabin, the only dwelling place I know of here. I want to rest. I will meet you there later."

"When? May I go back with you?"

"Go? You want to? Go with me now?'

"No, not really. I'd like to explore and learn more about the land and people here."

Then Alice remembered the figure of the old woman and asked John, "What about the woman I saw when we were landing from the ship? I would like to talk to her."

"I don't know. I have never seen nor talked to her. I see now that you point her out to me but I am tired. I want to return to the cabin."

"Wait…What…"

"No" John said emphatically. "I must go."

He starts up the hill toward the cabin, leaving Alice alone with Amir.

4. Exploring the Island

Amir approached Alice after John departed for the cabin.

Alice commented, "I have never felt so alone. I am pleased you are here."

Amir asked, 'What about the woman you have seen? "

"It is time for me to climb the hill to find her. I will continue until I reach her and find out more about her."

Amir warned Alice, "The trek is difficult because the hill is sandy and there is no path. With every step you take you will slip back half a step. But once you endure the hike you will reach the old woman you seek. You should carry this jug of water for the difficult journey."

Alice took the water and said to Amir, "I must go. I will somehow get to her despite the difficult challenge it presents. I realize it is something I have to do by myself. Amir, your guidance has been wise and it has enabled me to get to this point of going on alone. I am grateful. I hope someday we will be together again someday; but for now I must leave."

This step for Amir was a familiar one for being a guide usually involved this transition. It came with sadness at the departure but also understanding that it was part of the journey of self-discovery he had encouraged Alice to leave on the pier. Both Alice and Amir appreciated the bittersweet parting. Amir reached into the pocket of his vest and took out a gold coin. He handed to Alice, saying, "This is a Florin, a coin of gold originally from Florence in the 1200s, the principle exchange for the developing economy—significant to the development of Western Civilization as we know it. "

He went on to talk about what the metal represented. "Gold is a symbol of purity and often accompanies search for Truth and Purity. I give it to you as a talisman to keep with you as a reminder of my part in the beginning of your search for your sacred place. It represents the alchemy within your soul and is a symbol of the alchemy of the transformation of our relationship. I hope you keep it with you."

It was a bittersweet parting, each having grown fond of the other but part of the association was based on Alice finding her personal sacred place within herself. She had to do that independently. There would be the help of strangers along the path but ultimately she had to walk alone.

Alice turned and started walking up the hill, leaving the dinosaur behind. Amir was correct; there was no path and the ground was sandy. Every step she took Alice slipped back a little. After struggling a few hundred yards, Alice stopped to rest. She dug her toe in the sand and drank from the fresh water she carried. She slowly left her handprint in the sand and watched water from the jug wash it away as if it had never been there.

Alice realized the walk up the hill was far more difficult than she expected, even after the admonition from Amir.

Close by to where Alice rested on the hill she saw two knights jousting. Alice wondered why they were there. Then she realized the island had attributes from antiquity and they were knights to protect morality, right and wrongs. Alice realized that if she needed protection they were there for that. But Alice felt she did not need them. She had courage to complete her quest. However, just as having the company of Amir, the presence of the knights on the island was reassuring.

Suddenly one of the knights fell off his horse and was trying to get up. The horse ran away up the hill and seemed frightened. Alice got up quickly putting her jug of water down and ran to the aid of the fallen knight. As she reached the knight and as she was helping him up, she saw the horse turn and start running down the hill toward her and the knight, who was dazed and did not realize the danger he was in.

Alice pushed him out of the way, away from the direction the horse was approaching. The horse kept running and passed both people. The other knight came to Alice and his friend and got off his horse, tying its reins to a tree branch, thus securing his horse preventing it from causing danger.

Just then two more knights who had seen what happened from a short distance away rode to the knight who had fallen and was rescued by Alice. One rode to the frightened horse and grabbed its reins and waited quietly until the delinquent horse was calm.

The three knights and Alice waited until they decided the injured knight would be able to ride with one of the other knights temporarily. One of the knights asked Alice if she knew how to ride a horse. When she said she did, they offered her a horse to ride the rest of the way up the hill.

Reaching the top of the hill, Alice got off the horse. No longer being needed, the horse disappeared down the hill back toward the other horses and knights. Alice thought of the irony of protecting her protector. She felt even more confident of her ability to have good instincts and to deal with challenges quickly and effectively.

Walking across a short road, Alice saw a short, dark woman. Obviously not the wise old woman she sought. Alice wondered what diversion was in store for her and walked over to the woman whom Alice suspected was Mayan to find out more of what was in store for her.

5. Meeting Mayan Teacher

Alice observed the woman she assumed to be Mayan. She was short and stocky with graying hair but still tinged with black. She wore a long tunic in a bright color with a skirt underneath and wore sandals. She appeared to be about 60 years old. She had a jug of water balanced on her head and stood still as if waiting for Alice to approach.

"Hello," Alice said.

The woman did not answer.

Alice asked, "Would you like some water?"

She replied with a Latin accent in English, "I have quite a lot of water in the jug on my head."

Alice asked, "Who are you?" No response.

Alice continued, "Can you tell me anything?"

The woman answered slowly and deliberately. "You will learn a great deal here. People only come here who are able to leave things behind, otherwise they would not have the freedom to get on the boat and travel here."

"What is this place?" Alice responded, glad finally the woman was giving her information.

"This is the new land formed by past ages."

"Who are the knights?"

The woman replied, "They are from King Arthur's Court and the Crusades. They search for the Holy Grail. If only they would stop fighting over right and wrong they would discover it."

"What will become of them?"

"I don't know. Perhaps they will go on struggling forever."

Alice asked, "What is your name?"

That is a secret just as I cannot tell you yours. Only the goddess can do that."

"I know my name."

"That is your name from the other shore but not what you shall be called here."

Alice looked perplexed and confused. The woman went on, "You will understand. You have only just arrived."

"I cannot understand completely what you tell me. And what is even more perplexing I cannot see clearly your facial features."

"When you can you will know much more about yourself. You must become accustomed to our air, and to learn to hear and see in this place."

"Am I dead?"

"No. You have simply landed in the new most ancient world where there is an intermingling of past, present and what is foretold for the future. It is all contained within the moment, the Now.

"In this place there is represented what is best of human experience and knowledge throughout time. What is found here is distillation of what has been learned through trial and error of human experience. It has been determined to survive and be passed on from antiquity to the generations to inherit what has been bequeathed by ancestors."

"What about the place I have come from?"

"That will be with you always as part of your heritage. It is not lost. Just now you need to concern yourself with this new island and what your experiences here teach you. Perhaps for you will bring them back to the city you have left."

Alice commented, "This place is very lovely—but foreign to me."

For the first time the woman smiled and added, "Of course, you have just arrived. It will become more familiar. You will learn from it and much more will become clear as you travel further and encounter more teachers."

"You are saying many things that will take me awhile to understand. But there seems no hurry. I feel like I have a lot of time to adjust. Can I come back and talk more with you?"

The woman thought a moment and said, "We will have many talks. But you will learn many points of views. You will have to bend with the wind and respond to the sea for you will be exposed to differing ideas. For example, there will be a wise man near the church. You will learn many lessons from him but not all. It would take many ages for that."

Alice was feeling tired and her head was spinning. She felt like she had come a long way. Just then a little kitten appeared from behind a tree. Alice picked him up and suddenly felt a burst of energy and that she could continue the walk across the crest of the hill.

The Mayan lady smiled down at Alice holding the kitten and Alice felt a surge of warmth for the woman. Alice felt she could be enfolded in the skirts of the older woman. But Alice knew the woman would not let her. The Mayan woman was kind but stern. Alice hadn't sensed any humor from the woman's presence but guessed she would show it when Alice knew her better.

As Alice readied to go on the woman added, "You are right to search for the goddess you call the old woman. She will reveal much of what you want to learn and to become. You have shown courage in following you instincts to come with your guide and to seek the wisdom awaiting you from your encounters here but most especially in seeking the goddess.

"But I must prepare you for the task before you that you must accomplish before gaining audience with the goddess

"Only then will you be able to find the answers to the questions you came seeking in taking the journey here .For all to be revealed to you in meeting with the goddess you must write a statement of your mission here and validate that you have learned the tenets indicating your worthiness to enter the garden where the goddess dwells. She teaches the knowledge of the inspired and you must be deemed ready for your final transformation. Only then will you realize your dream and enter the center of your own existence."

Alice became little intimidated and asked, "How will I do that? Will you instruct me exactly what I will have to do?"

The Mayan woman nodded her head and responded, "You will go on father on this path and come upon a church where you will encounter a wise man called Doug who will instruct you of important basics for entering the presence of the goddess. It will then be your responsibility, after he indicated you are prepared, to enter the church and present orally your testament of what you have learned from your experiences since arriving on the island. It is also required to have some idea of what plan you might have to execute implementation of those lessons in your life upon undergoing the changes you seek."

Alice wondered exactly how all that task would be played out in actual writing and what was required to be expressed. She realized that to the woman was instructing her another next stage of her journey.

"Doug will tell you when you are ready to begin writing your reflection to be presented orally and partly in writing. He will introduce you to the scribe who dwells within the church. He will acquaint you with the skill of working within the scriptorium to accomplish the project you will have to create. All shall be revealed as you continue on your pilgrimage. You shall be guided along the way."

Alice was curious as to how all the Mayan woman had told her would come to be but reluctantly began to turn to leave. Before sending Alice away to continue her journey, the Mayan woman told Alice if she continued in the direction she had seen the goddess, she would come upon the wise man named Doug waiting at the church. He would reveal what were the tenets she was ready to learn from him.

Upon completing the course of education from him, he would direct her to the scribe dwelling in the church.

The monk would instruct her about the writing of her testament requiring indication she had accumulated the wisdom worthy of an audience with the goddess.

Once Alice submitted her writing to Doug and he accepted her mastery of the knowledge gained from her experiences after embarking for the island, she would be able to continue to the garden of the goddess.

"The wise woman" would be the facilitator of Alice's ultimate transformation, the realization of her calling to realize the manifestation of her unique sacred place within she sought.

Alice had listened to the Mayan woman, and comprehended what was in store for her, but Alice still could not understand in detail the complete nature of the woman standing before her. Perhaps, it was as the woman said, that understanding would come eventually as Alice went about completing her quest.

With that knowledge, Alice knew her time with the woman was complete and it was time to continue to the church where the wise man was to be her next teacher. Still carrying her jug of water and the gold coin Amir had given her, she thanked the woman for her kindness in imparting information. Alice bid the woman good by, sad at leaving the one who had revealed so much of what was in store and had shown her so much patient explanation.

Alice began to realize in making this journey there were also painful partings—with Amir, with John, and now with this teacher.

6. Important Lessons

Walking across the crest of the hill was much easier than the climb up because there was a path and the ground was level and less sandy. Alice enjoyed it as a beautiful walk lined with flowers and shrubs among the threes. She passed Indians she now knew were there to protect her along her way to find the goddess.

Alice stopped awhile to rest, to drink from her jug of water and to reflect on all the Mayan woman had told her she would encounter next. She wondered abut the wise man the woman had mentioned.

Having rested under a tree Alice was ready to continue her journey. She passed the knights still jousting and wondered if they would ever surrender their swords and discovers an end to their self-imposed struggles. The knights scarcely noticed her and Alice was too tired to stop to watch them or understand them. She reflected the irony of how she had protected the "protectors." The thought did not linger long with her because she saw the spire of the church and focused on reaching the church. She hoped finally to find the wise man she was expecting on her way to the sacred ground of the goddess.

When she saw the angel John had spoken of Alice knew she had arrived at the cabin near the church where John had sought refuge. Alice saw no sign of John, which disappointed her a little because she wanted to share all she had encountered since he had left her with Amir.

But while she was reflecting on that, she saw a man younger than what she had expected of one referred to as "the wise man." He sat resting in a chair near the door to the church with his eyes closed and appeared to be sleeping or meditating. His relaxed demeanor struck Alice.

Alice stood quietly near him and as she did so she looked down the hill into the valley below. In the distance she could see the landscape of the city she had left. In the landscape of the shore of the city she thought she could see the outline of her children, Angela and Jaime, and the dog, Sadie, running on the beach. Alice began to feel relieved they appeared to be doing well and hoped they would all soon be reunited.

But it still seemed right for that moment they were still in the city and she could pursue her solitary quest. Alice waited for the man to acknowledge her.

Everything was as it should be and all in its proper time. Looking back on the land Alice had left she realized how far she had traveled and experienced.

Looking ahead Alice could see the old woman a short distance away, surrounded by trees, flowers and grass.

At that moment, while Alice grew impatient with the delay of waiting for the man to awaken, he did. Alice was relieved to have him greet her. She wondered what was in store from her encounter with him.

He spoke in a quiet, gentle voice and said he was named Doug. He began by explaining that in waiting for him she had accepted the delay and indeed had accepted him on his terms. He went on to develop his point that one of the key aspects in finding peace is accepting people, things and events as they are.

Often, he explained, in attempting to force our will and expectations on situations as they are presented to us we respond with anxiety and anger. There comes a sense of relief and freedom in simply accepting reality as it is presented.

He explained, "If we are not feeling responsible for having to impose our expectations on what we experience, there comes relief and a kind of freedom. Immaturity manifests in wanting situations or others to be the way we want them. In realizing we are only responsible for our own welfare and ourselves, maturity comes into play. The only thing we can really change is our response or reaction."

Alice thought back to the world she had come from and all the time she struggled and resented all around her, She realized that might have been a waste of time and energy.

Perhaps she could have better invested her effort into determining how to improved her life despite having encountered difficult circumstances.

Doug went on to develop his point by suggesting forgiveness is an adjunct to acceptance. He made the familiar point that forgiveness is not forgetting, and we must not allow hurt or disrespect to continue. In the strength of finding the abundance of forgiveness in the universe for others, for situations, even for other countries, is overwhelming to realize. Especially to accept forgiveness for ourselves—to stop being judgmental and critical—is a grace to be appreciated profoundly. Alice thought of the nagging guilt she had in leaving her children. Suddenly she realized that perhaps leaving them was wrong but she had done what she felt right at the time.

But then she entertained that there was the possibility that she could rectify her decision by reconciling with them and being better at nurturing and protecting them from the challenges she had encountered growing up in the city. As a result of the lessons she had been shown she would present better alternatives. Alice felt deeply forgiven and the guilt and shame that had haunted her dissolved.

Doug was presenting fundamental tenants simply but profoundly. Alice was stunned by the impact his quiet words had on her whole perspective of how she had experienced her life. She began to view situations—particularly in her time growing up in the city—differently. Her point of view of her experiences there became more objective toward what had been done to her and what she had done to others as well.

All the anger and resentments spent on blaming and finding fault with others seemed energy misspent. The concept of forgiveness for all led to a profound sense of relief and made her break into sobs having a sense of deep absolution from her past failings.

Alice waited until she became calmer and realized it was time to consider leaving Doug. In preparing to leave Alice clung to him a few moments hoping he understood the depth of gratitude she felt from hearing his lessons—so profound but so gently delivered. A whole new door had opened for her but she had also closed one, which brought quiet and peace.

Alice waited for Doug to indicate the next step of entering the church to undertake the test with the scribe. She wanted to find out exactly what would be required to be in the presence of the goddess.

Doug stood and walked with her to the door of the entrance of the church. When Alice approached the front of the church, she could see figures carved in the walls surrounding the doors. She imagined them to be icons of significant leaders in the development of the formation of the culture of the island. And she knew they must be of the ancient times alluded to by people whom she had encountered while on her travels in the island.

Doug opened the door to the small church built of wood and reflected the rustic ambiance surrounding it. At the opposite end if the aisle there was a sparsely decorated altar. Behind the altar there was a large window with light streaming into the church. On the right side of the altar was an open door. Alice could see a white middle-aged man, evoking quality of character by his apparently balanced physical and mental demeanor, sitting at a bench. He was wearing the habit of a monk of the order of St. Peregrine, whom Alice knew to be the patron saint of cancer but also of pilgrims.

He was sitting at a raised bench, slightly slanted to facilitate writing and drawing. Doug explained the monk was Brother Edwin, a monk who was a scribe. In the scriptorium was another bench at right angle to Brother Edwin's. There were pens and paints appropriate for inscribing and illustrating sacred manuscripts used in spiritual practices and ritual.

Brother Edwin put down the pen he was using and stood up. He smiled at Doug and Alice as he approached them, reflecting a warm, welcoming demeanor. He greeted Doug, and turned to Alice and said, "I understand you have traveled here to seek an audience with the goddess. You are on a quest to come to the center of your own existence by relying on the guidance of strangers. In accomplishing this you hope to become worthy to meet with the goddess. In order to have revealed resolutions for questions for which you have made this pilgrimage, you have to find answers to the mysteries of your existence.

"You must write a testament of the journey you have taken. But before presenting the written document to Doug, you must orally report the lessons learned from your guides along the way, and how they have impacted you. Then add how you intend to implement these lessons.

"Now Doug will leave you with me now. But once you have completed the oral review and done the writing, he will review it and determine if you are worthy of having an audience with the goddess."

Doug was standing silently by the side of the small room. He went to Alice and told her he would return once Brother Edwin indicated she had completed writing a testament of her experiences. If he deemed it satisfactory, she would then be able then to proceed to meet the goddess in her sacred garden for the completion of the circle of her transformation.

Doug embraced Brother Edwin, and then Alice, assuring them he would be just outside the church in the place Alice had first met him to wait indication from Brother Edwin Alice had completed her tasks.

7. Reflecting

After Doug left, Alice looked at the bench awaiting her and she was daunted by the colored pencils and paints. She turned to Brother Edwin and asked, "Will I have to use the colored pencils and paints? I have not done well at that before."

Brother Edwin smiled and gently touched her shoulder. "No, Alice, you will not have to illustrate your manuscript. It is important for you to concentrate on writing and to include as much as what you have experienced as possible. To facilitate that, I am going to have you go back to the apse of the church to reflect on your journey. You have been getting illumination of your soul all during your life, not only here but also in the city. Now I want to examine your conscience deeply for insight into your responsibility in facing trials and accomplishments, in revelations occurring during you pilgrimage. All life is a meditation, a reflection of our connection and our relationship to what we refer to as

'GOD.' Once you feel you have done that, I want you to return here. I will help you in preparing your oral presentation and for writing your manuscript. Then Doug will return and evaluate your summary of events leading you to this point. If he finds it satisfactory, you will go on to meet the goddess. Do you understand what is expected?"

Alice was pleased that at last she was beginning to understand what she must do to meet the goddess. Alice was actually relieved to have time to think about what she was to write and to reflect on the spiritual mystery transpiring in her life. Alice nodded to Brother Edwin and entered the main part of the church and sat on a chair in the apse near the altar.

Alice looked in front of her and saw a beautiful stained glass window with the mosaic of a beautiful while dove surrounded by multicolored glass window through which the light from outside illuminated it. It appeared the dove was captured in a giant prism.

Alice reflected on the human mystery that was called God. Alice began to think of her life, realizing that throughout she was the common thread in her former experiences. She thought of the past and people who had influenced her and left their handprint on her life as part the destiny that brought her to this place. Alice particularly thought of those who had died and were no longer part of her life in the city. .She had mixed emotions—appreciation for all they had shared with her but were no longer part of her life. They had taken time to teach her many things and shown affection to her—rare in her time in growing up in the city but nonetheless at times present in her development. It had helped form the courage to embark on the boat. She had the insight that it was all part of her present experience, the past and what was to come in encountering the goddess. It was all in the present, what is "Now."

The beginning of what she was going to write began to form in her mind. She thought of the city she had left and her children, Angela and Jaime, she had left on the shore and who waited for her return. Amir had come into her life just then, encouraging her to board the boat, begin the adventure she had contemplated for so much of her life. She wondered about the reoccurrence of John appearing in the city and then again on the island. What impact would that have in the total outcome of her quest?

She thought of the irony of protecting the protectors that were the knights, the service she had performed in rescuing the fallen knight, then the opportunity to have his horse enable her to reach the top of the hill. The Mayan woman had waited with the instructions to go on to Doug sitting by the church in which she now contemplated it all. The memories all existed in the same moment, were all part of her present experience. At once all transcended humanity and the common theme in all was the presence of what was called "God."

Alice had the revelation that that which was called God was within her. The past, present and what were to come were part of eternity and existed now, in the present. Heaven, hell, all that people spoke of as distant were actually happening now. The present, the Now, is part of eternity expressed in the moment of what happens as we experienced it and that is what is called God.

Alice sat stunned by this realization and looked into the bright colors surrounding the dove. She was looking at the image of inspiration, the Holy Spirit of the universe as she experienced in the moment.

Gradually Alice became aware that Doug was waiting outside for her to express all this in her manuscript. Brother Edwin also waited to instruct her in the mechanics of inscribing the testament that would gain her entrance to the garden of the goddess. Alice then became anxious to pit all her revelations in the church and that leading up to them on paper, to express the wisdom she had gained allowing her to undergo finally the transformation sought.

Alice took one last look at the window, the dove surrounded by light and color, knowing that memory was forever imprinted on her soul. She carried now knowledge that assured her of the existence of God and that it was all within her as she experienced the eternal present.

Alice stood up and slowly left the sanctuary of her revelations and moved toward the door leading to the scriptorium where Brother Edwin waited to help in the next phase of her pilgrimage.

She saw Brother Edwin at his bench with a fine brush with blue paint at he tip, carefully painting sky as the background of a landscape at the edge of the page of a manuscript. She knew he had been waiting for her return from the church so she walked directly up to him and announced, resolutely, "I am ready to write."

Brother Edwin looked up and saw she was determined to begin the final test of her quest. She was ready to articulate her summation of what she had experienced not only on the island but upon her life before leaving the city as well.

Brother Edwin put his brush in a holder and stood up. He took Alice to the bench prepared for her and indicated she should sit at it without saying anything. Then, once she was seated comfortably, he said, "These pens are for you and there is plenty of paper. Write all you want and in as much depth as you desire.

"You have had time in the church to reflect. You have met many teachers and had an eventful experience on the island so you have much material to write about. Take your time; feel free to scratch out and start over. Make sure your thoughts reflect what you intend. If you have any questions, I am here to help. But this is your document and it is to be a complete statement from you. Do you understand?"

Alice did and was ready to begin putting down the thought that had been coming to her since entering the church.

Alice began to write.

8. Testament

When Alice had finished making an outline of the oral chronology of her life experiences and the written manuscript forming her apology to be admitted to the goddess, she told Brother Edwin she was ready to be examined by Doug.

Brother Edwin asked if she were certain she had completed all she wanted and Alice said she had done her best to be complete. Brother Edwin went outside and brought Doug into the scriptorium. Doug said he wanted to examine her privately in the church. So they walked together back into the apse of the church and Doug sat facing her, as she stood in front of the altar. Alice stood, with her notes for the oral part of the recital in her hand. She placed the manuscript lettered, in the manner taught her by Brother Edwin, on a table near the altar. Alice began to speak, clearly and emotionally.

"The beginning of my life—the alpha of my life—was in a city filled with cruelty and oppression. There were guards to insure the dictated path was followed. Yet not only did I survive, I found a way to go underground—to appear to conform to the dictates of the community, but in my own mind feel freely what I determined to be true for me and to find ways to lay the foundation for the person I am becoming.

"I felt pain and anger in not having the opportunity to express what I really thought I wanted to be. But somewhere during that time, some part of me held onto the faith, the belief that someday I would become free to express all I was suppressing in order to escape punishment.

"I was never completely annihilated. Perhaps the overseers of the city assumed I was following their ways, but I kept struggling to find my own way, my own version of Truth—the source of my life and the course it should take.

"I lived that dual life for many years, always believing someday I would break away from the conformity I wore as protection. But I stayed with what was familiar, what I was used to, until my children were born.

"Then it was time to confront the ways that had caused me so much pain. Those ways had fostered so much rage in relating to the world. I could not allow my children, Angela and Jaime, to grow up with the oppression to which I had been exposed. I could not guarantee they would be able to find their own internal resources to survive the ways of the city I had brought them into. I feared I had given them the gift of life only to pollute their expression of evolving into the destiny each should determine for themselves. I believed childhood is the basis for learning and being given the tools to master adulthood.

"Childhood, ironically, is the foundation to overcome childhood and evolve into surrendering it to maturity. The mind of a child is an embryo of intellect that challenges the world of the father and builds one not unlike that of the father.

"If I permitted my children to witness that I was accepting the world they perceived, I could not take the risk they would passively accept the unacceptable.

"Somewhere I heard: 'Suffering hones the soul for Bliss.' And I believed that to be true. Joy comes in redemption of exchanging pain for peace. I had to follow my dream to leave the city and sail to the island I could see in the distance. I had to take the chance I would find a better way for myself and for them in making the journey, even if it meant leaving them behind for awhile.

"One day, I decided it was time to walk down the hill of the city to the harbor and embark on the ship to take me to the island. I was afraid. I was leaving the familiar; I was leaving my children behind for the first time. I knew they were too young to understand what

I was doing. But I was at the midpoint of my life and it was time to allow myself to become the individual I had secretly nurtured and believed eventually would manifest.

"I walked to the shore, and suddenly a Blue Dinosaur joined me and offered to become my guide. It was a gift freely given, not sought or expected, but at that moment, needed. I went with the dinosaur named Amir and we arrived in a land filled with the beauty of nature that had been absent in the city. Then we were joined by John, also from the city on a quest similar to mine, and we shared similar experiences and were both on a difficult, extended quest.

"Each of us, in our separate ways, found compassionate teachers and guides. Each of us had different goals—in detail. I wanted to find the goddess I had seen from the boat; John wanted to explore the forests and interior of the island. But each of us had the same purpose, to find the Grail that was the wisdom of knowing God.

"I did service by protecting the fallen Knight, then I rode his horse to the top of the hill to find the woman of the earth, the Mayan woman who gave me the guidelines for continuing my journey. I found a young man, Doug. Wise beyond his years, he talked to me of acceptance and forgiveness. Suddenly I understood the anger and blame I had felt in the city was misspent and had continued my pain. I accepting what had surrounded me, and forgiving the abusers I could have maintained my dignity and found expression of reaction that would have brought me less pain. I could have adjusted my response to the oppression."

Then Alice paused, waiting for a response from Doug. But Doug gave no indication of his reaction to what she had said, and asked to see the manuscript. He took it and began to read her written works aloud.

"I found forgiveness not only for others I perceived had harmed me, but the miracle of God in the Universe is that the Abundance of mercy includes it for myself. And it is never ending—limitless. I cried at the recognition of that. The shame and guilt I carried so long was lifted from me and I could breathe freely.

"That brought me here. I sat in the church and had the realization that all that had transpired was my journey. It was MY LIFE. And the source of that, in the past, present and carrying me forward, is the source of life I chose to call God. There is a God and it is in me, and it is in the Eternal Now.

"I am ready. I know in my heart that is what I waited for in my childhood, what I sought in coming to the island. What I will bring back to the city, to my children, has come to pass. It is now. I am ready to meet the goddess. It is time to complete the Circle, the 'Wheel of Life.'"

Doug thought a few minutes. Alice felt his consideration was endless and grew restless. Then Doug, in his gentle and even voice, said, "Alice, I have determined you are ready to meet the goddess. You may leave to continue your journey, the completion of your quest. You may say goodbye to Brother Edwin and follow the path to the garden of the goddess."

Alice felt relief beyond words, grateful to Doug and to all who had contributed to that moment, the culmination of her education preparing her for the audience with the goddess. The lessons had come not only on the island but from her whole life experience. She simply thanked Doug and, after thanking Brother Edwin, left the church and began making her way toward the garden of the goddess.

9. Transformation

The walk away from the church was refreshing and Alice processed all the wise man had told her. While she walked Alice settled into anticipation of meeting the tall woman who was referred to as goddess.

The woman was not standing but sitting in a comfortable armchair facing the direction Alice was walking toward her across a cleared space in a garden filled with flowers and butterflies.

The woman began to speak in a strong but soft voice with clear distinction. When Alice approached she smiled and said, "I have waited for you for a long time. I have watched your long journey."

The goddess had long white hair piled on the top of her head. She was slender but looked strong and athletic. She was the sort of person about whom it is commented, "she grows younger everyday," as if she was moving backward in the right direction. In observing her, Alice realized her gently lined face was relaxed and peaceful but also alert and her eyes seemed to take in everything around her. Alice felt really seen, not only physically but in all the nuances of her appearance, emotionally as well as physically, internally as well as her outward appearance.

From that experience of being really seen, Alice had the realization that suddenly the image of the Mayan woman began to become clear. She could remember the earthen features, the nobility of character. "I know the texture of her clay." Alice remembered hearing somewhere. The Mayan woman had known, and even told Alice, eventually the physical clarity would happen. Alice found it all absolutely amazing that as her mind cleared all around her came into better focus.

In seeing the women clearly, Alice realized her own physical appearance needed to change. The dark, drab clothes she had worn from the city she had left behind were no longer appropriate for the person she was becoming. As if sensing what Alice was sensing, the Goddess reached behind her chair and picked up a large package and handed it to Alice. The goddess explained that the time had come for Alice to wear colorful clothes reflecting her newfound freedom and positivity from her experiences on the island.

Alice opened the package and discovered an array of fabric of many different bright colors and patterns befitting her new outlook. It all reflected the positive energy evolving in her personality. The negative perceptions were no longer present or relevant to how she presented herself. She knew she had to leave her old costumes behind. Alice heard herself saying aloud—to herself, to the goddess? "I don't need them anymore. I only know a time is ending for me and it took me to find this land, to come to this island, to a new frontier and to stop there—to look back."

Alice looked down the slope of the hill to the shore where there was the ship back at the island shore. She could see John going back to the old land. What had transpired for him after going back to the cabin and leaving her with Amir? Alice knew someday she would find out but she did not dwell on that. This was her time—her own transformation and discovery. John left with the memory of the old clothes she had worn—no longer needed and, at the moment, irrelevant.

Alice looked into the face of the goddess and said with determination, "I want to go to the spring and wash off all the dirt, to be clean."

Alice walked to a large pond behind the place in which the goddess sat. It was in a grove of trees. Alice put down the jug of water and the gold florin and removed the clothes she wanted to leave behind. She walked into the water. Alice felt a surge of joy and she felt reflections of experiencing faith.

Alice had a surge of memories, and reflected to herself something she had once written, "Faith enters my heart and warms my soul. It comes from within and unites with the universe. It comes in quiet moments and bursts of energy. I can soar by watching birds fly into the dawn. It comes in moments at midnight while swimming in a lake surrounded by mountains below a canopy of clear stars on a warm night. I wish I could sing the glory of peace that comes from faith. It is peace beyond joy."

In that moment, she realized "However much I struggle, it is all worth the moment that comes from the end of stress and strife. It is all unspeakable to the world—but exists deep within. I believe the struggle makes sense, a certainty I cannot fully understand but know to be true."

Alice remained still for many minutes, holding onto the feelings emerging from her experiences coming together since entering the garden of the goddess. Then, slowly she walked out of the pond, dried herself off and put on the new, colorful clothes given her by the goddess. She picked up the jug of water and placed the florin in a pocket of her dress.

Alice, with a new sense of self confidence, walked back to the goddess and sat on the ground near the old woman.

The goddess represented all the wise women Alice had known. They had just sat patiently waiting for Alice's time to come. They respected the silence—the silence that had brought her to that moment of realization. Alice began to cry because she had reached a destination and did not even know it until that moment. And the goddess knew the initiate was coming and wisely waited patiently, for the arrival of the one on a quest.

For Alice it was when the last piece of the puzzle fell into place. It takes a moment to look at the competition—to admire it, a moment to feel proud of it before scrambling it or putting it away and starting on a new one.

The goddess began to explain what was transpiring. "The elements of earth, air, water and fire are present in this moment. You bring fire—to join the water you have just cleansed with, the air around us and the earth on which you sit—because you were born under the sun of Sagittarius, a fire sign. The stars are at a point that at this moment the stars are aligned in the universe indicating your time has come.

"In the world there are dualities—man and woman. Good and Evil, sin and atonement—there is duality in almost every aspect of our existence—and you have indicated you understand that in your testament. Through your lessons the dualities you encounter are becoming integrated and balanced. The most significant integration is your realization of time—the circle of past and future, completed in the present, Now."

Finally the goddess spoke to the woman before her, "You have come to the time you shall be called by a new name. It is the name you bring from the women who are your ancestors and have lived with it in strength and courage. You are Clare."

In that moment Clare realized all that time she had been carrying the jug of water. She had carried the jug of water all that way. Clare put it down between herself and the goddess.

Suddenly it seemed important to get rid of the old clothes. She was impatient to do so. In the moment of discovery it all came to that, at the right time. How does it happen everything is in the right time she wondered?

She put down the water.

She put down her old clothes.

She put down—her life. She put it all down and stood there.

Clare exclaimed, "I am myself. I am creative. I am bright. I am competent. I am happy. I am sad. I am angry. I am calm and sometimes I am silly.

"I am.

"There is so much to learn but it starts with leaving clothes behind. The jug of water behind. The Indians and dinosaurs were protecting me all along. They served me well. All the time the knights were fighting for the rational level of my soul—but it was fruitless, irrelevant to what was most important."

There were no questions—there would be later—but not then at that moment.

That was a moment when thinking seems irrelevant. What next? Standing still and waiting.

10. Alice Going Home

Eventually Clare became aware of her surroundings again and realized her life had changed. She had completed her journey of discovery on the island. It was time to go home. She knew she would follow John back to the city she had left in such despair. She knew it was time to put into practice what she had written to gain access to meeting with the goddess and to discover from a new perspective the land she had been born into and had been her home most of her life.

She did not know what was waiting for her at the end of the Voyage back to the city. But she had gained courage and knew she could meet challenges awaiting her there. In the process of learning the lessons presented on the island she had developed confidence and was willing to implement the examples of compassion and service that had been shown to her.

Clare knew the goddess recognized part of the hero's quest involved ending the journey and returning to the place where she began. She looked forward to implementing changes learned or experienced in the process of searching for meaning or resolution of challenges.

The goddess stood up and moved toward Clare, "You have done well here. You have followed the path set out for you diligently and with completion of all your teachers have presented to you. Clare, you have shown imagination and intelligence in comprehending your lessons here.

"You are ready to return to the city and to find what your destiny is to be there now. I send you back with my blessings and appreciation for all you have accomplished in this island in this short time. The peace you have found here will stay with you because it has become an integral part of yourself. Even in the place you came from, which was difficult for you and caused you to leave, you will find new perspective and understanding in what will confront you.

"You have learned the importance of acceptance and forgiveness and that will alter how you experience differently the land to which you return."

Clare knew she was not the same person who had boarded the boat with Amir and that the goddess was correct. Nothing would ever be the same again but she had left to change and to alter the life she had before leaving. Now it was time to discover what the residents of the city had become.

Clare lingered a moment, sad at leaving the goddess who had been the agent of the culmination of her transformation. It was a bittersweet parting, just as it had been in leaving Amir. But Clare knew it was time to leave and Clare turned and started down the hill toward the harbor where she, like John, would embark to return to the place of origin in the same ship that had brought her to the island.

The ship waited at the dock, sails still furled. As Clare boarded the ship, she was aware of being alone. She missed the company of Amir and wondered who he was acting as a guide for now and knew whoever it was, they were in good hands. She thought also of John and wondered if she would again be joined by him after her sea journey—this time back to the city of origin.

Clare realized in being alone going home, her experiences on the island had given her self-confidence. She felt ready to meet the challenges awaiting her upon her return. She thought of Angela and Jaime, hoping they would understand and accept her absence. Clare knew she was now prepared to offer them more positive life alternatives.

Clare mused about what projects she would undertake to improve the quality of life for the residents of the city. She also wondered about needing courage to face her place of origin and to take on her role as a community organizer for the betterment of the environment. Clare found a seat near a balcony and found a piece of paper and a pen left in her purse from the scriptorium. She began to write to focus on her thoughts of her newfound courage.

"Peace comes in tiny steps of courage—courage to express life, to be individual and at one with a force that is life. It is not being afraid to look within and find at the core that which is within everything that exists. Whatever the outward appearance—however different—there is something that all share—person or thing. Even the smooth pebble has something in common with me. We share existing in this time and place. We transcend our differences."

That knowledge brought Clare peace, in that moment she realized yet again we are all part of eternity, the underlying force that is Love. Clare accepted that knowledge of that in silent moments brought her peace. Life moves in spirals—above and below, inward and outward, but in the movement, the dance, there is stillness at the center. And in that quiet, still movement, Clare found ineffable peace. Clare also knew that peace gave her courage. That courage would make her path to improve conditions of the city possible. Her determination to implement the experiences of her quest on the inland would become complete in her return to the place that, in the past has caused her so much pain and suffering. Culture evolves and she knew she would become an instrument of the evolution of the city.

Clare had heard somewhere "Our life evokes our character." Clare vowed to herself, during the voyage home, to rise to the occasion of meeting the challenges awaiting her.

Clare watched the swelling of the sails diminish as they were lowered to approach the shore of the city. Clare was home.

As Clare disembarked, her heart leapt. There was John on the shore waiting for her. When she approached him, he hugged her and said, "I knew you would return. So I have met every ship returning from the island since I returned to the city hoping you would be on it. Finally, here you are."

Clare was so filled with joy to see John waiting for her. She had hoped to learn of his journey upon reaching the church on the island and had seen him embarking on the ship to return to the city when she entered the garden of the goddess but finally they could talk and share reports of their journeys after leaving and going separate ways on the island.

John suggested they go to a coffee house to talk, not only about what had happened on the island but the life John was experiencing since returning to the city.

They sat outside at a café near the pier. John explained he had become a gardener. He tended plots of residents of the community and also was helping create public parks in the city; He had developed an interest in transforming garbage to compost as part of filling the need for fertilizer in his work.

He lived in a community of people who had also made the trip on their own quests to the island and returned to form a New Age Community and chose to live in a commune. He told Clare her children were living in that house, as he watched over them awaiting her return. They were well and happy—looking forward to being with her again.

He was full of news of the wonderful unfolding of the new spirit in he city. There were farmers growing produce in the fields outside the city, merchants selling minor crafts needed by the residents of the town, bankers helping create an economy that would provide financial security for those in the work force—following their bliss in contributing their part of the economy.

Then John quoted Martin Buber in describing the ambiance of those living in the city. "The encounter, the dialogue, the relationship—the Highest of Joys." Then their eyes met.

John and Clare, who had left the city, shared time on their separate difficult and extensive journey—shared in a quest—recognized that hey had shared an intimate goal each found them realizing they were from the same cloth and were part of the one they had each found in their path.

John reached out and touched Clare's hand and staring into her eyes told her of the love he had had for her since seeing her heading to the boat that first day.

Clare reflected on the goddess's words about duality and integration—male and female. Their relationship had come full circle. The omega.

John let go of Clare's hand and said that in the commune there was a man called Haskill whose bliss was preparing wonderful meals. It was time for dinner and Angela and Jaime would be waiting for their mother. Clare could share a wonderful meal, prepared with the produce from the farms, shared with her new family, in her new home.

When Clare and John walked toward the house along streets lined with trees and flowers, Clare talked of her hope to create a school for children to explore and learn about math, science, history, religion but most of all she wanted them to develop their creativity and find the source of each child's bliss. She wanted to follow the guidelines of classical education reflected in English and German schools she had heard about and were the model in the United States for Friends School, Quaker Schools stressing the importance of integrating athletics, education and service—all pursued with diligence. There should also be education for adults without examinations or papers where adults could learn a little about a variety of subjects. Clare told John about an early Renaissance man of many interests and talents named Leon Battista Alberti who had originated the idea of education for children which inspired classical education throughout the western world, including the Quaker Schools.

Then they arrived at their destination. Angela and Jaime with Sadie, the dog, ran out of the house to embrace their mother who had been missed. The pain of time apart dissolved in the joy of reunion and the knowledge they had come to a better time.

The wheel of Life spiraled into a new level of peace beyond joy.

Afterword

The experience of accepting Joseph Campbell's challenge to write my personal myth has been an experience of discovery. I have learned a lot about the mechanics and requirements of what should be included in the structure of myth, as well as the characteristics of the development of the Hero. This has been a process of self-awareness and appreciation of my life history and of alternate ways of viewing past incidents in my life especially in my formative years.

But the most rewarding aspect has been the collaboration with Toby and Matt, who have given of time, information and insights into their own examples of knowledge of myth and their experiences of their own life histories.

My sincere hope is that from reading my story readers will discover the book of *The Power of Myth* or watch the series of interviews of Joseph Campbell by Bill Moyers and be inspired and motivated to write their own personal myths.

Myth is symbolized by completion of the circle and as I write this my circle of completing my myth is complete. But in truth it is like a spiral, a circle going deeper at each completion of the circle, my life continues to unfold and evolve into all new adventures and journeys. I face these with newfound appreciation of all that has gone on before and with joyful anticipation of what is yet to come. But as I wrote in the discovery of the book, it is all experienced in the present, the Now. And as is indicated in the title of the book, may it all, with pain, suffering and challenges aside, be experienced in the Bliss of the opportunity existing in this Beneficent Universe.

Susan Clare Fratis Penny

Made in the USA
San Bernardino, CA
14 November 2018